WALTON -- JUL 2021

Please return this book on or before the date shown above. To
renew go to www.essex.gov.uk/libraries, ring 0345 603 7628 or
go to any Essex library.

Essex County Council

Puss in Boots

by Jill Atkins and Shahab Shamshirsaz

W

FRANKLIN WATTS
LONDON•SYDNEY

Once, there was an old miller
with three sons. Before he died,
the miller gave each son one thing.
He gave his first son the mill.

He gave his second son the donkey.

He gave his third son the cat.

The third son was sad.

He had no money.

How could he look after a cat?

"Don't be sad, Master," said Puss.

"You can talk!" said the miller's son.

"Yes," said Puss. "I have a clever plan.

But first I need some boots."

The miller's son got Puss some boots

and a hat.

"For my plan to work," Puss said,

"you must pretend to be

the Marquis of Carrabas."

Next day, Puss took some rabbits to the king's palace. He bowed to the king. "These are a present from my master, the Marquis of Carrabas," said Puss. The king was pleased.

Every day, Puss took presents to the palace. "From the Marquis of Carrabas," he said.

One day, Puss heard some news.
The king and the princess would soon
be passing by.
"Quick," said Puss. "Get in the river."
The miller's son took off his clothes
and dived in. Puss hid the clothes.

"Help!" cried Puss. "Robbers have stolen my master's clothes."

The king sent servants to fetch some new clothes. The miller's son put them on. He looked like a real marquis!

"Come, Marquis," said the king.

"Ride in my coach."

When the miller's son and the princess
saw each other, they fell in love.

"But I am too poor to marry
a princess," thought the miller's son.

Puss ran ahead. He saw some farmers.
He told them, "If the king asks you
who owns these fields, you must say
the Marquis of Carrabas."

Soon, the coach came along.

The king asked the farmers,

"Who owns these fields?"

"The Marquis of Carrabas,"

replied the farmers.

"Is that your master's castle?" the king
asked Puss. "I would like to visit it."
"Of course," said Puss. "I'll go and get
everything ready."

The castle belonged to a mean giant.

Puss had a plan to trick him.

"What do you want?" roared the giant.

"Is it true that you can turn into different animals?" asked Puss.

"Yes," replied the giant.

And he turned into a lion.

"Very clever," said Puss.

"But can you turn into a mouse?"

"Yes," replied the giant.

And he turned into a mouse.

Puss gobbled him up.

Just then, the coach arrived.

The miller's son led the king

and the princess into the castle.

"What a beautiful castle," said the king.

"You must be very rich."

The princess and the miller's son
smiled at each other.

Very soon, they were married.

And they all lived happily ever after,
especially Puss.

Story order

Look at these 5 pictures and captions.
Put the pictures in the right order
to retell the story.

1

Puss took presents to the palace.

2

The miller's son and the princess
were married.

3

The miller's son got some boots for Puss.

4

The miller's son jumped in the river.

5

Puss told the giant to turn into a mouse.

Guide for Independent Reading

This series is designed to provide an opportunity for your child to read on their own. These notes are written for you to help your child choose a book and to read it independently.

In school, your child's teacher will often be using reading books which have been banded to support the process of learning to read. Use the book band colour your child is reading in school to help you make a good choice. *Puss in Boots* is a good choice for children reading at Turquoise Band in their classroom to read independently.

The aim of independent reading is to read this book with ease, so that your child enjoys the story and relates it to their own experiences.

About the book

The miller's son is very poor, but he does own a very special cat. Puss is determined to be rich, and he has a plan.

Before reading

Help your child to learn how to make good choices by asking: "Why did you choose this book? Why do you think you will enjoy it?" Look at the cover together and ask: "What do you think the story will be about?" Ask your child to think of what they already know about the story context. Then ask your child to read the title aloud.

Ask: "Do you think the cat in this story is going to be special in some way? If so, what do you think might be special about him?"

Remind your child that they can sound out a word in syllable chunks if they get stuck. Decide together whether your child will read the story independently or read it aloud to you.

During reading

Remind your child of what they know and what they can do
independently. If reading aloud, support your child if they hesitate or
ask for help by telling the word. If reading to themselves, remind your
child that they can come and ask for your help if stuck.

After reading

Support comprehension by asking your child to tell you about the
story. Use the story order puzzle to encourage your child to retell the
story in the right sequence, in their own words. The correct sequence
can be found on the next page.
Help your child think about the messages in the book that go beyond
the story and ask: "Why do you think Puss found it so easy to trick
the giant?" Give your child a chance to respond to the story: "Did you
have a favourite part? Did you like the ending of the story?"

Extending learning

Help your child understand the story structure by using the same
sentence patterning and adding different elements. "Let's make up
a new story about Puss. What might he want this time, and what plan
might he come up with to get what he wants?"
In the classroom, your child's teacher may be teaching use of
punctuation marks. Ask your child to identify some question marks
and exclamation marks in the story and then ask them to practise
reading each of the whole sentences with appropriate expression.

Franklin Watts
First published in Great Britain in 2021
by The Watts Publishing Group

Copyright © The Watts Publishing Group 2021

Series Editors: Jackie Hamley and Melanie Palmer
Series Advisors: Dr Sue Bodman and Glen Franklin
Series Designers: Peter Scoulding and Cathryn Gilbert

A CIP catalogue record for this book is
available from the British Library.

ISBN 978 1 4451 7400 6 (hbk)
ISBN 978 1 4451 7401 3 (pbk)
ISBN 978 1 4451 7402 0 (library ebook)
ISBN 978 1 4451 8151 6 (ebook)

Printed in China

Franklin Watts
An imprint of
Hachette Children's Group
Part of The Watts Publishing Group
Carmelite House
50 Victoria Embankment
London EC4Y 0DZ

An Hachette UK Company
www.hachette.co.uk

www.franklinwatts.co.uk

FSC
www.fsc.org
MIX
Paper from
responsible sources
FSC® C104740

Answer to Story order: 3, 1, 4, 5, 2